PRESIDENT

Written by Natalie McDonald-Perkins

Illustrated by Mary Ibeh

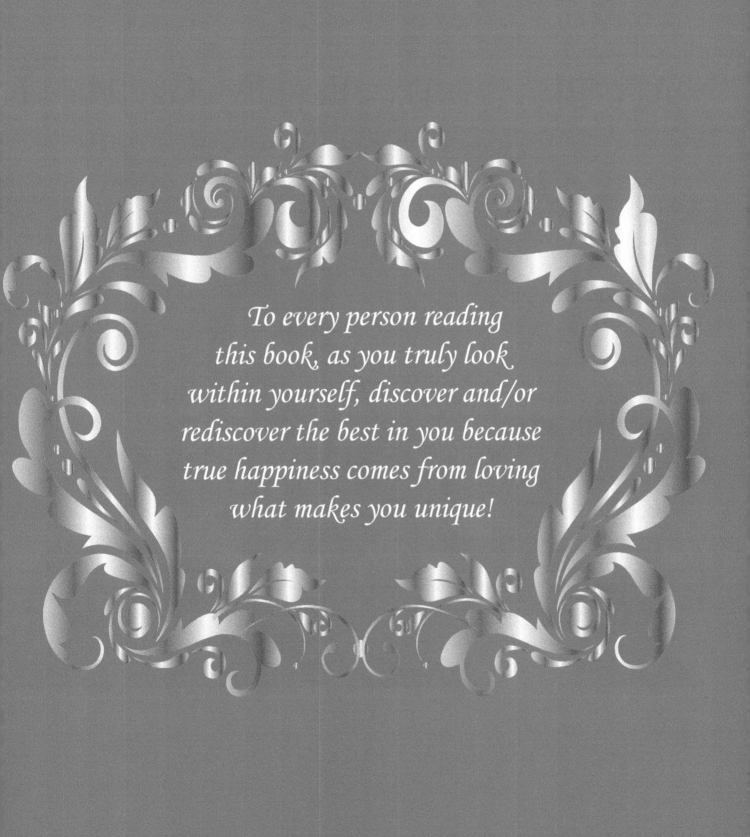

To every person reading
this book, as you truly look
within yourself, discover and/or
rediscover the best in you because
true happiness comes from loving
what makes you unique!

Mrs. Patterson, the school counselor, has created a group for students who are bullied at school. The students have learned how to use "I" messages and assertive language. Today, Mrs. Patterson is excited to see her students, in their last counseling session, being more confident and happier than ever. She has an interesting task for them.

"Good morning, everyone," Mrs. Patterson welcomes the class.

"I want you to write a poem that describes what makes you special. If you want, you can share it with the class."

I AM BRAVE
I AM STRONG
I AM ABLE
I AM CONFIDENT
I AM INTELLIGENT
I AM HONOURED

As the students get started on their poems, she hopes that each one of them will use their newfound confidence to read them to the class. Soon, it is time for the children to stop writing.

"May I read mine first, please?" Justice asks.

"Of course!" Mrs. Patterson smiles at her.

Mrs. Patterson knows that Justice is one of the more confident ones in the group, and she is glad that she has asked to go first. She knows her poem will inspire others.

As Justice stands up, nerves begin to fill her body. Her heart is beating quickly, so she takes a deep breath and imagines being her mama. Her nerves quickly disappear.

"'Your feet look like sailboats.'

That's just one of their jokes.

I used to cry and just tell my folks,

'My big feet are keepers.'

I wear Mama's shoes and pretend I'm one of the teachers.

I look like my mama with all of her cool features!

Filling her shoes is my dream.

I'll be like her one day.

I don't care what they say.

I'll reach my goals.

I proclaim this today!"

All the students clap for Justice. And they hoped they could be just as brave as her.

Riley? Would you like to go next?" Mrs. Patterson asks gently.

"Um, yes." Riley takes a while to get to the front of the room.

She has always been incredibly shy and nervous because she struggles to read clearly.

Riley can feel all eyes on her. She thinks of her new friend, a dog named Brownie.

She knows her friends are just as loyal as Brownie. They won't mind if she mixes her words up.

"I didn't like to read out loud when the teacher called my name.

Words that I see, and words others see,

They aren't always the same.

Reading was not my only challenge.

Math is also a pain; 87 is 78.

I wanted to blame my brain,

Until I met my Brownie boy, who never judges me.

I can read all day at my own pace.

He makes me feel so free!

My reading makes him smile again,

And wag his tail side to side.

Reading is my superpower because it makes Brownie have joy inside!"

"Aww!" the children say. Everyone is so proud of Riley, and they don't mind that she read more slowly than others. More importantly, Riley is proud of herself!

Mrs. Patterson notices Someina walking to the front of the classroom without saying a word.

"Oops, I forgot something," says Someina, as she rushes back to grab her eyeglasses. This is the first time that Mrs. Patterson hasn't had to remind her to put them on.

Today, she is able to clearly see the words that she is going to read and all her friends' smiling faces that reminded her to be courageous.

"They laughed at my glasses.
So, I hid them in my desk.
I couldn't see the board.
Then I failed my science test.
My teacher told me to put them on.
But I didn't think I looked my best.
When I put on my glasses,
I can learn without the stress.
I am distinguished,
Not shy.
Now my parents are proud.
Because my grades are rising high!"

All of the poems so far are so inspiring that the other students can't wait to share theirs. They play Rock, Paper, Scissors to decide who will go next. Ray is the winner.

It isn't simply speaking that makes Ray uncomfortable. He is also nervous about sharing how he feels when people make fun of him for being short. Standing amongst the people who care about him within the classroom, makes it easier for him to share. He goes to the front of the classroom and stands as tall as a statue.

"I was embarrassed when they would call me 'Shorty.'

Now, I don't really mind because my personality and brain bring me all the glory.

I can play sports and run like no other.

I love my height.

I got it from my mother.

I'm always in the front row of a class picture,

Smiling with glee.

I count on my resilience and sportsmanship.

My height doesn't define me!"

As Ray goes back to his seat, Mrs. Patterson notices Mario and Ray doing their secret handshake. They play on the same baseball team. Mario is usually quiet. Lately, he has been sticking up for Ray and being a supportive friend when people bully him.

It is Mario's turn. Mrs. Patterson has seen Mario participate in all the activities during the counseling sessions, but she doesn't remember him saying very much. Mario quickly heads to the front of the room. Mario thinks it's so cool that he speaks both English and Spanish. It is finally time to tell his friends why.

"I get teased because I have a distinguished lingo.

Habla Español.

That's how I communicate with my people.

I'm a proud Mexican!

See the snake and brown eagle?

I translate for my padres during my parent-teacher conference.

I always tell the truth, and I do it with confidence.

Instead of teasing me,

People should learn cultural tolerance."

The children are amazed by his pride for his language and country. And to top it off, they love the sound of his voice.

Soon, Mrs. Patterson sees Faridah coming up to read her poem. She remembers how difficult it was for Faridah to make friends because she doesn't speak very much. But when she does, her words catch everyone's attention. It is clear from the children's faces that they have lots of questions about her hijab.

As Faridah begins to read her poem, she can hear her jida, her grandmother, telling her, "Be brave, and tell those bullies what your hijab means to you!"

"'What's on your head?' they ask.
It's a hijab that I wear.
Don't care what they think.
Don't mind if they stare.
My friends always ask.
Me about my hair.
I comb it.
I wash it.
Let's just be clear!
I take it off when I'm at home with my family,
When I sleep, and when I shower.
Underneath my hijab,
My hair has a pin with a flower.
I love wearing hijabs with all of my attire!

All the students clap for Faridah, but her new friend, Sharonda, gives her a thumbs up, and then stands up herself. It is her turn to read.

At last, Sharonda goes to the front of the room, smooths out her shirt, closes and opens her eyes, then swallows. She is ready.

"I was born with Cerebral Palsy.

The whispers and the stares,

How they appall me.

No friends to play with at recess.

I begged my mom to withdraw me.

I am smart.

I am strong.

I can do what they can do.

Oh, the choices in life.

What shall I pursue?

I see myself in high places.

I know my dreams will come true!"

"That poem was wonderful, Sharonda! I knew you could do it!" says Mrs. Patterson with admiration.

"Thank you," replies Sharonda. Today is the first time she has ever spoken in public about what makes her different. And she doesn't regret her decision.

Jacquelyn's time has finally come. Mrs. Patterson remembers how frightened Jacquelyn was one morning when she refused to get out of her dad's car because she thought she would be teased again for wearing an afro.

Today, that fear feels like it's a million miles away as Jacquelyn stands confidently at the front of the class with her latest do.

"My cotton mane spreads like the sun's rays.

Oh, I love my natural hair!

People are welcome to stop and stare.

Don't you dare; never put your hands up there!

Afro, braids, and twists are the hairstyles I wear.

Proud to be African American,

With my fist in the air!"

24

Justice, Sharonda, and Ciara can relate to Jacquelyn because they wear similar hairstyles. They are proud of Jacquelyn for embracing her natural hair.

Ciara is last. The second Ciara reaches the front of the room, her dark chocolate skin, radiates as a beam of sunlight comes through the window. All eyes are on her, and she loves it. The attention and respect that she is getting at this moment makes her feel like a celebrity.

"People pick on me because I have a richness of melanin in my complexion.

With my skin, I see no imperfections.

Black is the color of a radiant diamond.

Diamonds are transformed coal.

I can't worry about what they say,

Because loving me is my goal.

I'm not just beautiful from the outside.

I have a beautiful heart, mind, and soul."

Faridah and Riley are very proud of Ciara. They've always known that Ciara is intelligent, well-spoken, beautiful, and a great friend.

"Thank you, everyone, for sharing. Because you have learned to embrace your differences, you understand the importance of being supportive and caring. You now have the tools that you need to face anyone who chooses not to see the best in you," Mrs. Patterson says proudly.

Justice raises her hand high in the air.

"Justice, would you like to share something with the group?" Mrs. Patterson asks.

"Yes, Mrs. Patterson. I learned that the **best in me** is simply being me," says Justice.

"That's right!" exclaims Mrs. Patterson.

"I'm not going to let anyone's words upset me anymore," Someina announces.

"That's wonderful," Mrs. Patterson says.

Sharonda speaks up. "I'm proud of being different."

"I'm proud of being different, too," Mario adds.

The rest of the children agree.

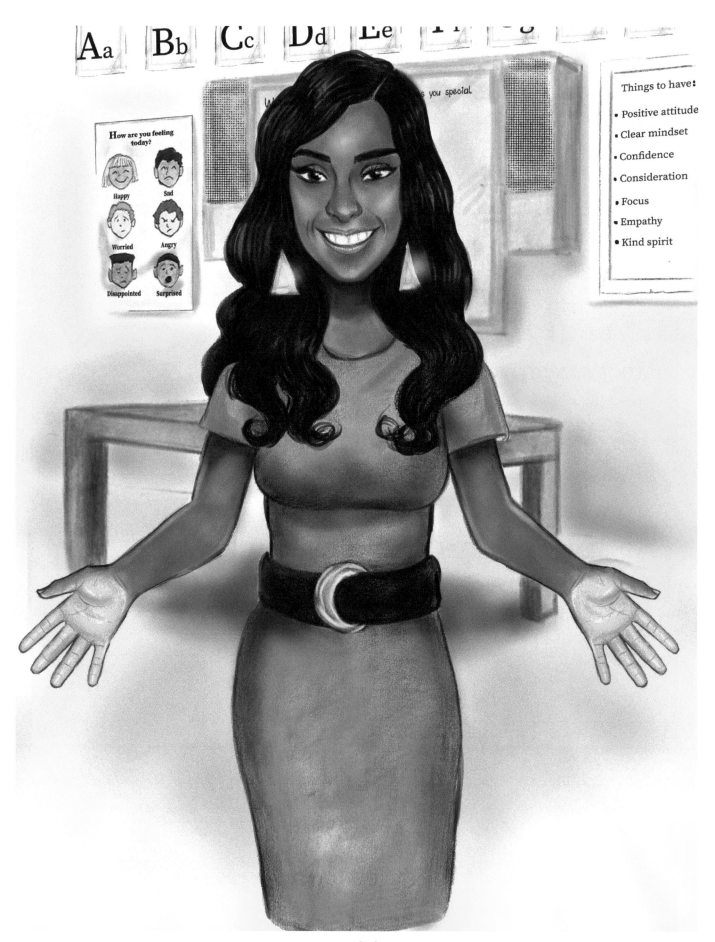

"And I am proud of you all!"
Mrs. Patterson says with a smile.

About the Author

Natalie McDonald-Perkins is an elementary school teacher from San Francisco, California. She earned her Master of Arts in Teaching with a concentration in Multicultural Studies, Social Justice Education, and Action Research from California State University, Fresno in 2015. Natalie has worked in the education field for 18 years and has been a teacher for seven years. Throughout her entire career, she has been dedicated to serving underprivileged youth. She spent most of her career teaching in Sacramento, California and East Oakland, California. Her professional interests include social-emotional learning, culturally relevant teaching, and behavior management through positive student-teacher relationships. She also enjoys mentoring and supporting other teachers with routines, rituals, curriculum, and instruction. In her free time, she enjoys writing, spending time with her family, and reading. The little girl in her desired more positive representations of African American boys and girls in children's literature. She is honored to gift you with "Best in Me," her debut book. Visit her website at natalieperkins.org.

About the Illustrator

Mary Ibeh resides in the United Kingdom. She has always been passionate about art and animation and has been drawing since she was a child. She studied Fine Art at Wimbledon School of Art, as well as Animation at Solent Institute in Southampton, England. She has worked in an animation studio in London, as well as a cartoon artist at the Chessington World of Adventure park in Surrey and the London Eye. She writes as well as illustrates children's books and stories. She also draws live caricature portraits at weddings, birthday parties, and special events. She is an avid reader, movie enthusiast, fitness aficionado, music lover, and content creator. Visit her website at https://www.cartooncreativecaricatures.com.

Family Dedication

First, I want to thank God for the support of my family and friends, resources, wisdom, and strength to write this book. I dedicate this book to my family. To my husband, Justin, your unwavering support is one of the reasons why I can finish what I start. I love you with all my heart. For my daughter, Justice, you are fearfully and wonderfully made. I have seen the best in you since the day you were born. You will always be my baby girl. To my Daddy (Ray) and my Mommy (Jacquelyn), thank you for encouraging individuality, giving me the freedom to speak my truth, and teaching me to respect and love others, despite their differences. To my big sister, LaRyta (Mrs. Patterson) aka "Ree Ree," thank you for being a part of my literacy story without even knowing it. I guess we can both agree that sneaking to read your Babysitter's Club collection wasn't so bad after all. To my nephews: Lamar Jr., Solomon, and Joël remember that through your leadership and discipline, you can help transform the narratives of African American men. To my big cousin, Sharonda, thank you for being brave and letting me share your story with the world. This book is in memory of my Grand Daddy (Joel) and Grand Mommy (Dorothy), who would say, "If you're bored, read a book."

Love,
Natalie ❤

If you enjoyed "Best in Me," leave a review on Amazon, Goodreads, and Facebook.

Visit natalieperkins.org.
Follow "Best in Me" on Instagram @bestinmebook and Facebook @bestinmelikepage. Also, stay tuned for the upcoming book "Proud to Be…"Your continued support is appreciated!

Thank you again,

Natalie McDonald-Perkins

CPSIA information can be obtained
at www.ICGtesting.com
Printed in the USA
BVHW022030190821
614611BV00041B/905